P9-DOD-909

King & Kayla

and the Case of the
Missing Dog Treats

Written by
Dori Hillestad Butler

Illustrated by
Nancy Meyers

Ω
PEACHTREE
ATLANTA

For Bob, because it's another book one

—D. H. B.

For Jane and Finnegan with love

—N. M.

Published by
PEACHTREE PUBLISHERS
1700 Chattahoochee Avenue
Atlanta, Georgia 30318-2112
www.peachtree-online.com

Text © 2017 Dori Hillestad Butler
Illustrations © 2017 Nancy Meyers

Edited by Kathy Landwehr
Design and composition by Nicola Simmonds Carmack
The illustrations were drawn in pencil with color added digitally.

Printed in October 2016 by RR Donnelley, China
10 9 8 7 6 5 4 3 2 1
First Edition
ISBN 978-1-56145-877-6

Cataloging-in-Publication Data is available from the Library of Congress.

Contents

Chapter One 4
Making Peanut Butter Treats

Chapter Two...12
Intruder!

Chapter Three......................................20
How to Solve a Case

Chapter Four.......................................30
Clues

Chapter Five 40
Case Closed

Chapter One

Making Peanut Butter Treats

Hello!

My name is King. I'm a dog.

This is Kayla. She is my human.

Kayla and I are making

peanut butter treats.

I LOVE peanut

butter treats.

They're my

favorite food!

"Sorry, King," Kayla says. "These treats aren't for you."

My tail droops.

"They're for my friend Jillian," Kayla says. "She just got a new puppy."

Kayla stirs the flour, oatmeal, and baking powder. She adds milk, eggs, and peanut butter. Then she rolls out the dough. It smells so, so good!

I wait for her to give me some of that dough. I wait…and wait…and WAIT.

I can't wait anymore. I say, "Kayla, please give me some of that dough."

She looks at me. "Do you want to go outside, King?" she asks.

"No," I say. "I want some dough!"

"I'll take you outside in a little bit," Kayla says.

She presses a cookie cutter into the dough. She lays the pieces of dough on a cookie sheet. Then she puts the cookie sheet in the oven.

"May I lick the bowl?" I ask.

"I know you want to lick the bowl,
King," Kayla says. "But you can't.
Raw dough isn't good for dogs."

She puts the bowl in the sink.

My tail droops even lower.

Ding!

Kayla takes the treats out of the oven.

She sets them on a wire rack to cool.

"Now we can go outside and play,"

Kayla says.

Chapter Two

Intruder!

Kayla throws the ball. "Go fetch, King!" she says.

Oh, boy! I LOVE to fetch. It's my favorite thing!

I run…run…RUN after the ball. I bring the ball to Kayla. She throws it again.

"Hi, Kayla! Hi, King!"
calls a voice from the back
porch.

It's Kayla's friend, Jillian!
"Hi, Jillian!" I call back.

Jillian is not alone. "This is Thor," she says.

"Hello! Hello! Hello!" Thor says.

Thor has lots of energy. We run. We roll in the grass. Thor nips at my ears.

"Please don't eat my ears," I say.

But Thor is just a baby. He giggles and nips at my ears again…and again…and AGAIN!

Sometimes it's hard to be the big dog.

"I need a drink of water," I tell Kayla. I also need a break from Thor.

I run up the back stairs and into the house.

Sniff...sniff...

I smell an intruder!

I don't see him.

But I smell him.

He STINKS!

I hear Kayla, Jillian, and
Thor clomping up the steps.

"There's an intruder in the house!" I tell Kayla.

She and Jillian walk right past me. They go over to the treats.

"King!" Kayla cries out. "There are three treats missing! Did you take them?"

"No!" I say.

But I don't think Kayla believes me. She looks at me like I'm a bad dog.

I don't like it when Kayla thinks I'm a bad dog.

Chapter Three

How to Solve a Case

"I didn't take the treats," I tell Kayla.

I look at Thor. He and Jillian came through the kitchen on their way to the backyard. Maybe Thor took them?

"I want my treats! I want my treats!" Thor cries. He leaps at the counter. But he's too short to reach the treats. So I don't think he took them.

Sniff...sniff... I still smell that intruder!
Maybe the intruder took the treats?

"Sit, King!" Kayla says.

I don't want to sit. "Let's find the
intruder," I tell Kayla.

Kayla doesn't understand.

"King!" she says. "I told you to sit!'"
She makes mad eyes at me. I don't like
it when Kayla makes mad eyes at me.

I sit.

"I didn't take the treats," I say again.

Kayla sniffs my face. She opens my mouth and looks inside. Thor looks, too.

"I don't think King took the treats," Kayla says.

I wag my tail.

"How do you know?" Jillian asks.

"His breath doesn't smell like peanut
butter," Kayla says.

Kayla is a good detective.

"If he didn't take them, who did?"
Jillian asks.

"We'll find out," Kayla says.

She grabs a notebook and pencil. "Let's make a list of everything we *know* about this case," she says.

1. There are three treats missing.
2. King was in the kitchen.
3. King's breath doesn't smell like peanut butter.

If I could write, I would add this to

Kayla's list of things we know:

"Now let's make a list of what we *don't know* about this case," Kayla says.

1. Was anyone else in the kitchen?
2. Who else likes peanut butter treats?
3. Who else could have taken the treats?

If I could write, I would add this to Kayla's list of things we don't know:

Who is the intruder?

Where is the intruder?

Did the intruder take the treats?

"Now we need a *plan*," Kayla says.

I have a plan:

Find the intruder!

Chapter Four

Clues

"Follow me!" I tell Kayla, Jillian, and
Thor. I put my nose to the ground.
Sniff...sniff...

"Are you looking for clues, King?"
Kayla asks.

"Yes," I say. I follow the intruder's scent
from the back door to the counter.

"Hey! What's this?" I ask.

It's a bit of toast.

I LOVE toast. It's my favorite food!

I gobble up the toast. Then I follow
the intruder's scent from the counter
to the hallway.

"Hey! What's this?" I ask.

It's a bit of peanut butter treat.

I LOVE peanut butter treats.

They're my favorite food!

I gobble up the—oh no! That bit of peanut butter treat was a clue.

You shouldn't eat clues.

I follow the intruder's scent from the hallway to the living room.

Kayla's mom, Jillian's mom, and Jillian's little brother are there. They are not intruders.

Kayla tells her mom about the missing
treats.

"Hmm," her mom says. She looks at me.

"King didn't take them," Kayla says. "His breath doesn't smell like peanut butter. Did you see anyone go into the kitchen? Do you know who could have taken the treats?"

The moms shake their heads.

"Come back here, Adam," Jillian's mom says. She picks up Jillian's little brother.

"Waaaaa!" Adam cries.

Maybe Adam took the treats?

"Hey! What's this?" I ask.

It's a hair. A gray hair. In fact, I count
one...four...two...eight...six gray hairs!

No one here has gray hair.
I follow the hairs to the couch.
I peer under it.

Two yellow eyes peer back at me.

Chapter Five

Case Closed

"INTRUDER! INTRUDER!" I bark.

The intruder is eating Thor's treats under our couch.

I need to chase him away. I need to rescue the treats. But I don't fit under the couch.

"Ha ha!" The intruder laughs at me.

"What's the matter, King?" Kayla asks. She and Jillian look under the couch.

"It's a cat," Jillian says. "Where did he come from?"

"He must have come in when the back door was open," Kayla says.

I paw at that cat. But I can't reach him.

"Ha ha!" The cat laughs at me again.

I need help. And I know who can
help me…

Thor!

He is small enough to fit under
the couch.

The cat lets out an angry yowl and
zooms out into the living room.

Thor and I chase him through the
kitchen and out the back door.
Kayla closes the door behind him.

"You were right, Kayla," Jillian says. "King didn't steal the treats. That cat did."

"Bad cat," I say.

"Good boy, King," Kayla says. "You solved the case of the missing treats. You are the king of crime solving."

"And you are the queen," I say.

Jillian gives Thor a peanut butter treat. Kayla gets me a piece of cheese.

Oh, boy! I LOVE cheese. It's my favorite food!

The End

Oh, boy! I LOVE books.
They're my favorite things!

More great mysteries from King & Kayla

King & Kayla and the Case of the Secret Code

HC: $14.95 / 978-1-56145-878-3

Kayla receives a letter written in code.

What does it say?

King & Kayla and the Case of the Mysterious Mouse

HC: $14.95 / 978-1-56145-879-0

When King's favorite blue ball goes missing,
he and Kayla must put together clues to figure
out where it went—and who has it.

King & Kayla and the Case of the Lost Tooth

HC: $14.95 / 978-1-56145-880-6

Kayla lost a tooth—but now it's missing.

Where did it go?